Out of Nowhere

For my friends,
whether near or far.

First published in 2020 by Nosy Crow Ltd
The Crow's Nest, 14 Baden Place, Crosby Row,
London SE1 1YW
www.nosycrow.com

ISBN 978 1 78800 838 9 (HB)
ISBN 978 1 78800 839 6 (PB)

Nosy Crow and associated logos are trademarks
and/or registered trademarks of Nosy Crow Ltd.

Text and illustrations copyright © Chris Naylor-Ballesteros 2020
The right of Chris Naylor-Ballesteros to be identified as the
author and illustrator of this work has been asserted.

A CIP catalogue record for this book is available from the British Library.

Printed in China
Papers used by Nosy Crow are made from wood grown in sustainable forests.

10 9 8 7 6 5 4 3 2 1 (HB)
10 9 8 7 6 5 4 3 2 1 (PB)

Out of Nowhere

Chris Naylor-Ballesteros

nosy crow

Once, I had a friend.

She arrived out of nowhere one day.
I asked where she'd come from, but she just didn't know.

She stayed with me and, every day, we shared
a picnic on the big rock looking out over the forest.

Then, at the end of each day, we would watch the moon come up together.

But one morning, I woke up and my friend
was nowhere to be seen.

I looked everywhere . . .

. . . and at last!

There was my friend — lost,
deep in the forest.

Now, I know I look very strong with my tough
shell and spiky horns. The truth is, sometimes . . .

I don't feel very strong at all.
But if I wanted to find my friend, I'd just
have to pretend.

I packed a very big picnic and set off.

I sang a song to myself to feel a little bit stronger.

I'm a beetle and don't you know?
I'm not afraid of a hungry crow.
Yes, I'm a beetle and can't you see?
Fearsome frogs don't frighten me.
Oh, I'm a beetle and, er . . . haven't you heard?
I'll keep singing till . . . till I run out of words!

No one bothered me much, so I think it worked.

And then, just when my big brave song
finally ran out of words, I was there!

But I realised I'd made a very big mistake.

I had no idea where my friend was.

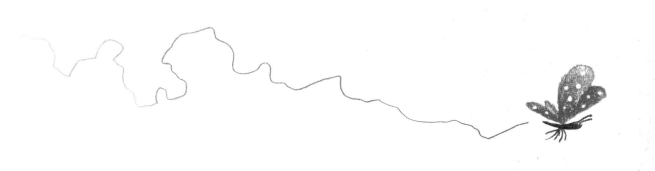

I was tired, and it was a very long way back to the big rock, so I decided to stay for a while.

Just until I got my strength back.

And then, out of nowhere,
someone suddenly arrived.

I felt I'd seen her before, but at first, I couldn't quite put my finger on it.

Then I looked more closely. And I just knew. It was my friend! She had changed a little bit but it was my friend all the same.

We shared my picnic, just like before.

We did the same the day after.
And the day after that.

And today too.
It's just like before, on the big rock.

Then, at the end of each day, we take off
to watch the moon come up together.

And my friend is with me again.

Out of nowhere.